Free
the
lines

clayton junior

Copyright © Clayton Junior 2016

First published in 2016 by words & pictures
Part of The of Quarto Group
The Old Brewery, 6 Blundell Street, London N7 9BH

British Library Cataloguing in Publication Data
available on request

ISBN: 978-1-78493-626-6

1 3 5 7 9 8 6 4 2

Printed in China

Free
the
lines

clayton junior

words & pictures

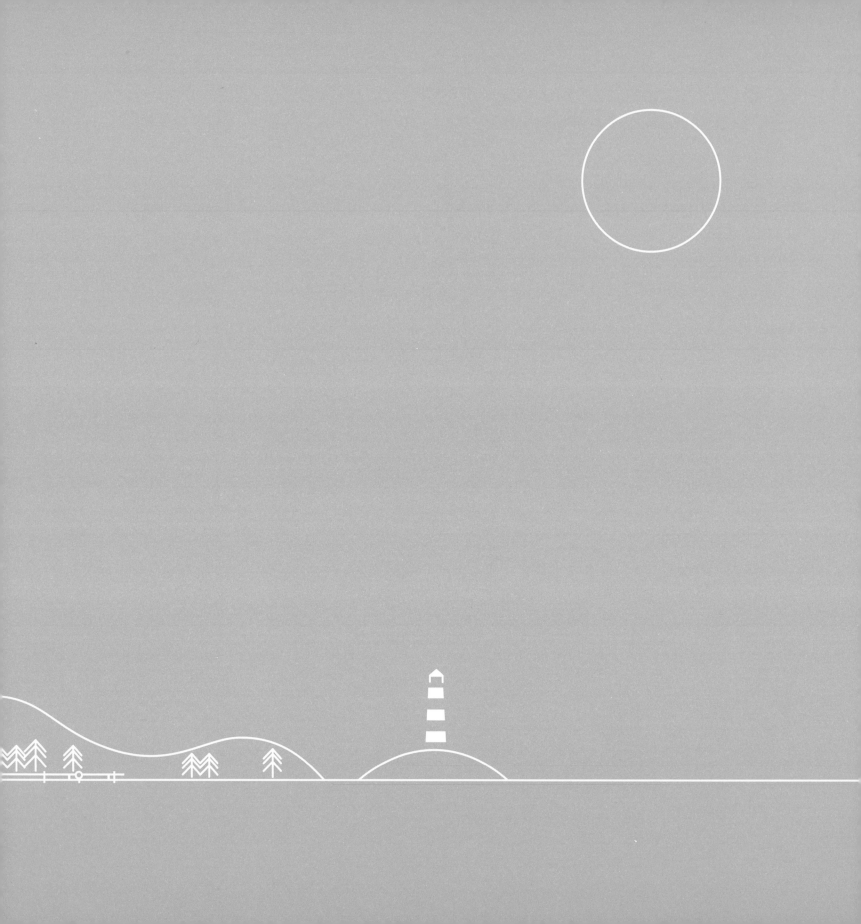

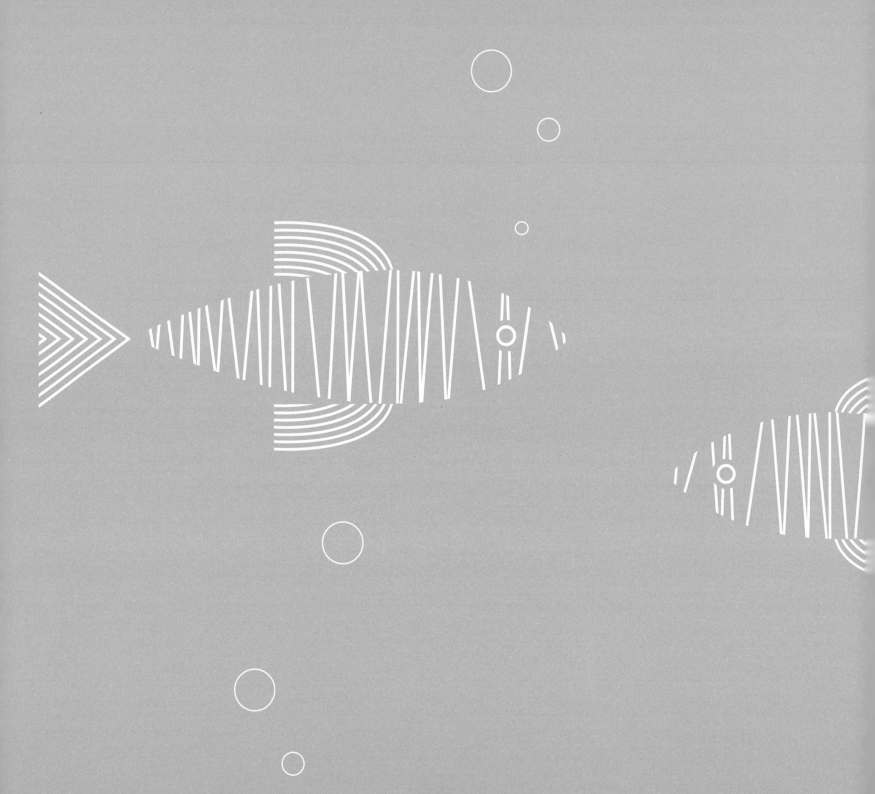

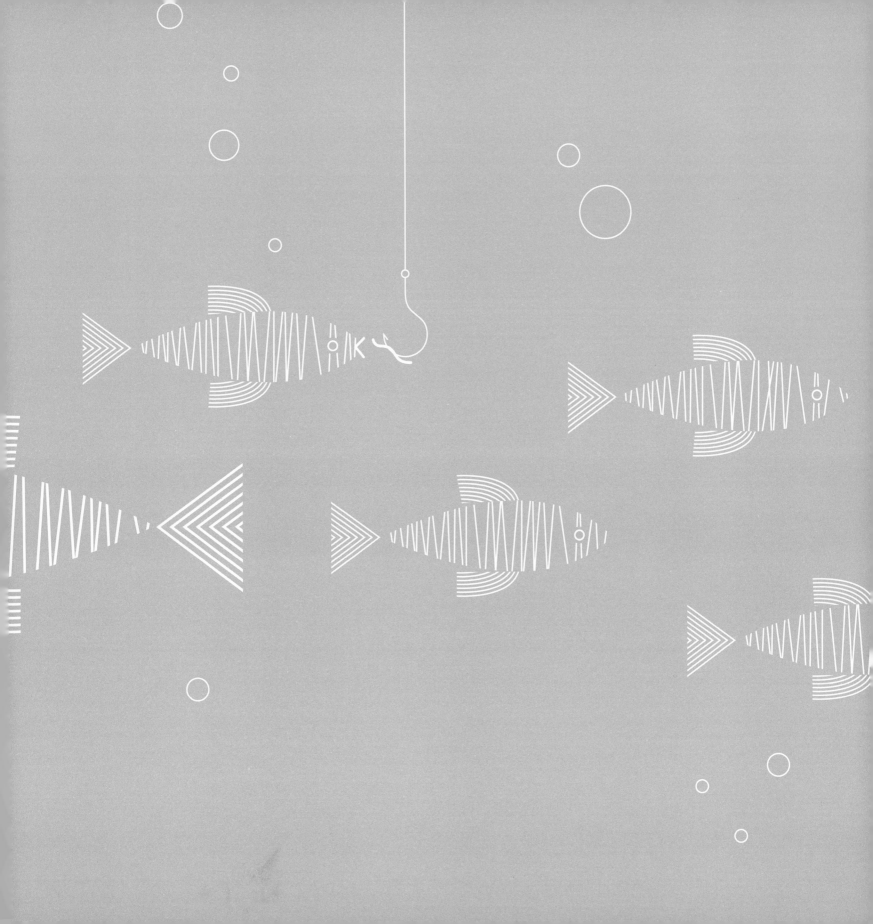

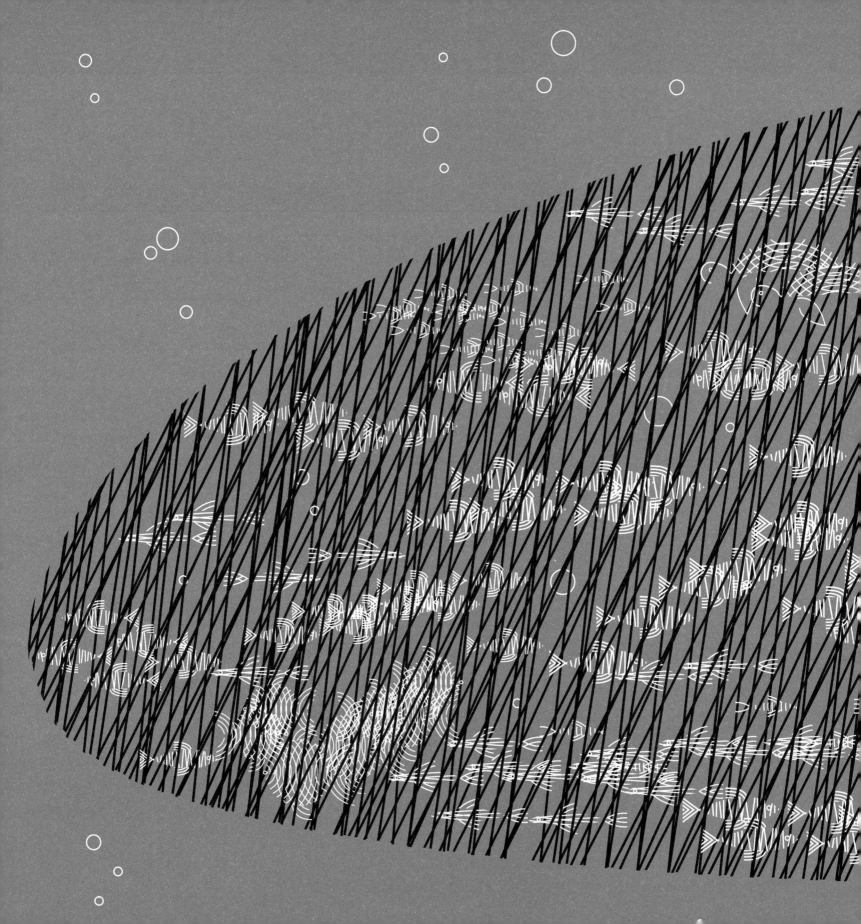

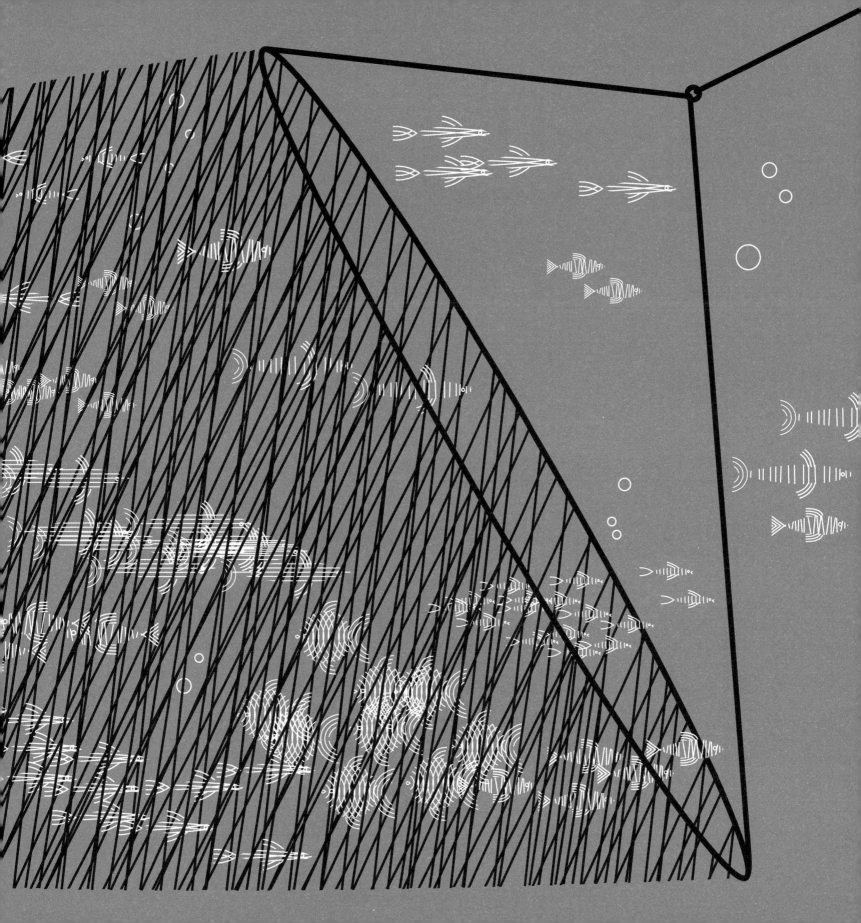